MS
JEB

FORBIDDEN
Friendship
by Judith Eichler Weber

OLD CHARLES TOWN LIBRARY, INC.
200 E. WASHINGTON ST.
CHARLES TOWN, WV 25414

SILVER MOON PRESS

98001545

FORBIDDEN FRIENDSHIP
by Judith Eichler Weber
Copyright © 1993 by Judith Eichler Weber

The publisher would like to thank Marianne Riello
for her help in preparing the Historical Postscript.

All rights reserved. No part of this book may be used or reproduced in any manner whatsoever without written permission except in the case of brief quotation embodied in critical articles and reviews.

For information contact
Silver Moon Press,
126 Fifth Avenue, Suite 803
New York, New York 10011.

First Edition
Edited by Judy Makover
Designed by John J.H. Kim
Cover Illustration by Nan Golub
Printed in the United States of America

Library of Congress Cataloging-in-Publication Data

Weber, Judith Eichler, 1938-
        Forbidden friendship / by Judith Eichler Weber. -- 1st ed.
        p. cm. -- (Stories of the States)
        Summary: In the late 1800's in Massachusetts when her
father brings in Chinese workers as replacements for striking
employees at his factory, Molly befriends one of the young Chinese
despite her mother's prejudice.
        ISBN 1-881889-42-4 : $12.95
        [1. Labor disputes--Fiction. 2. Chinese--United States--
Fiction. 3. Prejudices--Fiction. 4. Massachusetts--Fiction.] I.
Title. II. Series.
PZ7.W388Fo 1993
[Fic]--dc20   93-22572
                                                           CIP

STORIES OF THE STATES

TABLE OF CONTENTS

CHAPTER ONE
"There's Going to be a Strike!"

The knock at the door startled Molly. She stopped writing in her diary. "Are you awake, Miss Molly?" the housekeeper called from the hall.

"Yes, Beatrice," Molly answered.

"Breakfast in half an hour, Miss Molly," Beatrice said. Molly heard her repeat the wake-up knock on her younger brother Willie's door and finally on Betsey's door.

Rays of morning sun filled the peaked ceiling in Molly's bedroom in her family's home, Chase Hill.

Carefully, Molly blotted the date, April 4, 1870, in her clothbound diary. After dipping her pen into the ink bottle, she gazed out of her window at the Berkshire mountains, which circled the town of North Adams in western Massachusetts.

"How can I become a writer if nothing ever happens to me?" she wondered.

Molly was writing when the door opened and her mother entered the bedroom. "Molly, you'll be staying home from school today," she said abruptly. She was clutching a handkerchief, and her eyes looked red and swollen.

"Why?" Molly asked.

"I received a telegram from your father in San Francisco. He thinks it would be a good idea if you did not go to school," Mama answered as she dabbed her eyes. Before Molly could ask another question, Mama turned and walked out of the room.

From his bedroom down the hall, Willie was cheering the news of an unexpected holiday. Then Molly heard her sister objecting, "But, Mama, I have to go to school."

"You heard me, Betsey," Mama repeated firmly, as she shut the door to Betsey's room.

Mama was sipping tea when Molly came into the dining room and sat down next to Willie. Molly noticed that Mama's eyes were no longer red and she had dabbed powder on her fair skin.

"Is it the factory?" Molly asked, as she removed her napkin from the silver napkin ring.

"There's a problem," Mama said.

"What kind of problem?" Molly asked.

"It's not your problem," Mama sighed.

"But Mama, if I can't go to school..." Molly insisted.

"It's a business problem. Your father will handle it." Mama picked up a small roll and prepared it carefully with butter and jam.

"Mama," Molly pleaded, "I just want to know what's going on."

"It's the union. There's going to be a strike," Mama said hesitantly.

"What's a strike?" Willie asked, looking up from his bowl of hot cereal.

"The workers don't want to work for your father unless he does certain things for them," Mama said. "Your father doesn't want you and your sisters to go to school until he returns. And no one is to go down to the village either." Mama closed the conversation by lowering her eyes as she sipped her English tea.

Molly felt a surge of excitement. Good or bad, at least something was finally going to happen in North Adams.

After breakfast Molly decided to practice the piano. She was playing a Mozart minuet when Grandpa interrupted her. Molly was surprised to see him, since Grandpa usually visited only on Sundays.

"Molly, come into the library. We're going to have a family meeting." Grandpa Clark's face looked strained.

Grandpa was the mayor of Cheshire, a town about ten miles away, and he owned the general store. Since Grandma had passed on, he spent every Sunday at Chase Hill, always bringing with him a giant wedge of the famous Cheshire cheese.

Molly sat in a straight-back chair at the far end of the paneled library. Mama, Willie, and Betsey had already found seats, and Beatrice and Kevin, the driver, stood near the door.

Grandpa stood behind Papa's big oak desk. He was wearing a three-piece herringbone tweed suit, with his gold watch chain draped across his rather prominent belly.

He cleared his throat. "As you know, my son-in-law, Mr. Bartlett, has been away in San Francisco for the past two weeks. He wrote to me and asked that I talk to the family and staff.

"Mr. Bartlett thought it would be a good idea if you understood the reason for the strike. The trouble is in the bottom room, where the Wells pegging machines are."

"I thought the problem was money," Betsey whispered to Mama.

"Let your grandfather explain," Mama said.

Grandpa continued. "Thank you. The bottom room is where the bottoms of the shoes get stitched onto the tops of the shoes by machine. It's the only place in the factory where there are members of the Knights of St. Crispin union. Now every single man has walked out."

"But why?" Molly asked. "Papa has always treated them fairly."

"If you heard them talk, you wouldn't think so," Grandpa answered.

"What do they want?" Mama asked.

Grandpa took a piece of paper from his inside pocket and slowly unfolded it. The room was as quiet as Papa's factory on Sunday.

"One, they want an eight-hour work day."

Mama looked surprised. "But everyone works ten hours! That's a fact!"

"They want their wages raised from $1.70 to $2.00 per day, and the union wants the right to fire an employee if he doesn't pay his union dues," Grandpa went on.

"Even if he's a good worker?" Mama asked.

"I'm just reading their demands, Catherine. And finally, the union also wants the right to inspect the account books in order to adjust wages to profits."

Now Mama looked indignant. She rose before she spoke. "The Bartlett Shoe Factory is a privately owned company. Thomas will never open his books to outsiders."

Grandpa folded the paper. "Now, now, Catherine. Don't get excited. These are only the union's demands."

"What do you think Papa will do?" Betsey asked.

"Your father expected a problem, and he has a plan. That's why he went to San Francisco," Grandpa said.

"What plan?" Molly asked.

"Can't say." Grandpa stepped away from the desk, signaling that the meeting was over.

"Molly," Betsey whispered, "come into the dining room. I have to speak to you privately."

Betsey closed the door behind her sister. "I need your help. I can't stay home from school today," she said seriously. "I have to see Charles."

"Betsey, I'm sorry you have to stay here, but Mama said 'no school' because of the strike."

"I don't care about the strike! I just want to see Charles. Molly, you don't understand. I'm in love with him."

"I know," Molly said, and she smiled.

"How did you know?"

"Well, you're always talking about him and sometimes you blush when someone mentions his name," Molly answered.

"You could tell? Oh, Molly, I can't stop

thinking about him. Now that there's a factory strike, I'm afraid his father will forbid Charles to court me."

"Court you? How exciting!" Molly exclaimed. "But maybe Reverend Winslow would be right to object. After all, you're only fourteen, Betsey."

"In two months I'll be fifteen, and Charles is sixteen. We plan to marry when Charles graduates Drury Academy next June," Betsey said with assurance. "I'll be Mrs. Charles Winslow. And, remember—Mama married Papa at sixteen."

"Well, I don't want to marry so young. I want to graduate and maybe even go to Radcliffe College in Boston," Molly said. "I want to be a writer."

Betsey shrugged her shoulders. "Just wait till you fall in love, Miss Molly Bartlett. You're only twelve now. You'll change your mind." She sighed. "I just have to see Charles today! I miss him so much. I have to know if the strike will change our plans. Maybe now he won't want to ask Papa if he can court me." Tears filled her eyes.

Molly gently patted her sister's back. "Oh, Betsey, how can I help you?"

Betsey dabbed her eyes with a rumpled lace handkerchief, then she looked at her sister.

"I have an idea."

"What is it?"

"I'm supposed to meet Charles today after school at the gardener's cottage. We could ask Mama if we could go berry picking in the hills behind the house after lunch. Then I could meet Charles while you're picking berries."

"But your bucket would be empty."

"We could share the berries and just say the picking wasn't good. Please, Molly!" Betsey begged.

Molly paused. "All right. But I promised my piano teacher that I'd practice every day so wait a little while and then, when I finish, come down, and we'll both ask Mama if we can go berry picking together."

"Without Willie. He can't keep a secret," Betsey added.

The sisters hugged.

Molly raced through her scales and piano pieces. Her thoughts kept wandering to Betsey and her plans. When Molly finished practicing, Betsey joined her. Hand in hand, they walked into the library where Mama was writing a letter.

"May Molly and I go berry picking this afternoon?"

"Betsey, don't bother me now. I have too many things on my mind," Mama said impatiently.

Betsey looked helplessly at Molly.

"Mama," Molly broke in, "I finished practicing the piano, and I don't have any homework. May we go berry picking? Please!"

"All right, but not until after lunch," Mama said, as she continued to write.

Betsey smiled.

Molly's bucket was filled with berries as she walked down the narrow gravel path behind Chase Hill. She could see the back of her father's giant brick factory on the far side of the Hoosac River. The building was so big that it blocked Molly's view of the village of North Adams. Next to the factory were small, two-story wooden houses.

She spotted Betsey waiting behind the cottage. She was filling the berry bucket with stones and then emptying it, filling it and emptying it, again and again. It was well past the end of school.

"Betsey! Betsey!" Molly shouted from the path. "We have to go home."

Betsey turned and walked slowly up the hill. Molly didn't have to ask her sister about Charles. She could tell from Betsey's tear-stained face that he had never come to meet her.

CHAPTER TWO
"I Fear There Will Be a War in This Town"

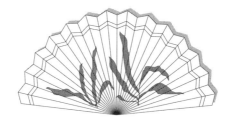

Five days later, Molly closed the door of her room after lunch and took her diary out of the night table drawer. She could hear her sister crying in the next room. Betsey had not heard from Charles since the strike began.

Molly tried to concentrate on her writing.

When our carriage arrived at the railroad depot to meet Papa, there was an angry crowd pushing toward the last two cars of the train. I could see scores of Chinese men peering fearfully out of the train windows. How scared they looked and how odd! The mob pressed forward, and it looked like they would overrun the constables. I heard cursing and there were even some bricks and vegetables hurled at the railroad cars. Photographers were tak-

ing pictures, and there was a lot of noise. Papa appeared on the train platform with a Chinese man next to him. I could see Papa's temper rising. Suddenly I saw him take his silver pistol out of his jacket. He let his hand rest at his side—but everyone could see the pistol. He spoke to the crowd. "I will protect my workers," he declared loudly. The crowd became quiet.

Then a line of short Oriental men started to emerge from the train. They were wearing little round hats, wide-legged pants, and oatmeal colored collarless shirts that were fastened down the front with "frog buttons," cloth knots that went through a loop on the other side of the placket. Their hair was pulled into a single braid that hung down their backs.

As the line passed our carriage, I looked at the men. My eyes met the dark brown eyes of one young man. He quickly looked away.

The crowd stepped back and made a path as Papa led the men into empty carriages and wagons. They drove to the factory. The men are going to live inside the building, where Papa has made dormitories and a kitchen. He doesn't think it will be safe for them to live in town.

Molly was interrupted by a knock at the door. She quickly hid the diary in the drawer.

"Molly, dear," Mama said, as she walked into the room, "your father and I have decided that the family should try to get back into a normal routine as soon as possible."

"Yes, Mama," Molly agreed.

"You and your brother and sister will be going to school tomorrow," Mama continued. Suddenly, she stopped talking. A pitiful sobbing was coming from the other side of the wall.

"What is wrong with your sister?" Mama's voice sounded concerned.

Molly didn't answer. She lowered her eyes and twisted one of her corkscrew curls.

"It's the Winslow boy, isn't it? Never mind. You don't have to tell me anything, Molly," Mama said gently. "I'll talk to Betsey myself." She left the room.

Molly didn't like keeping secrets from her mother. And she didn't like the idea of going back to school, either. She was afraid her friends wouldn't talk to her because their fathers were in the Knights of St. Crispin union and they would surely blame her father for the strike. Besides, all the exciting things were happening on Chase Hill and at the Bartlett Shoe Factory—not at school.

Betsey stayed in her room all day and skipped dinner. Molly knocked on her door twice, but Betsey told her she wanted to be left alone. Molly decided not to bother her again. She read Tennyson and tried to write a poem about the strangers coming to North Adams.

At dinner, Molly listened as her father said a prayer of thanks before their meal. It was their first family meal together since he had come back to North Adams.

"Thomas, you look very tired," her mother said.

Papa did look weary; his eyes had deep shadows under them.

"I am, Catherine. I've had a very disturbing time, and I'm certain there are more problems ahead for us."

"Please tell us about the train trip, Papa," Molly asked.

"It was long and uncomfortable. The other passengers hated the Chinese. They complained that they were evil and dirty. The truth be known, the two cars the Chinese men were in smelled a lot better than mine. The Chinese men washed every day and none of them smoked.

"Johnny Sing, the leader of the men, speaks English. He has proven to be most intelligent and helpful. It is only the language barrier that makes the others appear limited."

"Thomas, you sound as though you like these people," Mama said, a little surprised.

"I respect them. And you will, too, if you give them a chance. They're intelligent, frugal, and, if the reports are correct, efficient workers. They only wish to earn money so that they can go home and buy land in China or send for their families to come to this country."

Mama pushed her dish away and folded her napkin. "Thomas, I'm very upset at the way this strike, and bringing the Chinese men here, has affected all our lives. Merchants we have always dealt with suddenly won't touch our money, and I have been snubbed at my sewing circle. The children are afraid to go to school. We are prisoners on Chase Hill. I fear there will be a war in this town," Mama said firmly.

"Catherine, I think you are exaggerating. It's an uncomfortable situation, but it's not dangerous. When the factory is working again, and the men in the union have cooled down, everything will be forgotten. Life in North Adams will return to normal."

"I pray you are right, dear," Mama said.

Just then, the doorbell rang and Beatrice announced that the Reverend Winslow and Mr. Logan wanted to speak to Papa.

The men were shown into the parlor. Molly decided to sit in the music room so that she could hear the conversation.

Her father's back was to her, but she could

see the Reverend and Mr. Logan clearly. The Reverend was a big, heavyset man with a graying beard and thick black eyebrows that moved up and down when he spoke. Mr. Logan was a young teacher at Drury Elementary School. He had been a soldier in the Union Army and had lost a leg. Everyone liked the tall, lean teacher.

"I am against bringing in these Chinese men," the Reverend said, "but I cannot ignore the fact that seventy-five heathens are living in North Adams. We must educate them in Christian ways," the Reverend declared with assurance.

Mr. Logan looked uncomfortable. "I'm not a religious man, Reverend. I see it more as a practical problem. If we cannot communicate with the Chinese workers, then they will never be able to live in our community," he said.

"They will be here for only two years," Papa said.

"Perhaps they can make an economic differ-ence," Mr. Logan added. "They will buy clothing, food, and goods at our stores in North Adams."

"Yes, that's true," Papa agreed. "And I don't plan to board them for two years in the factory. I assume eventually they will want to move to room-ing houses."

"Reverend Winslow has approached me to start teaching English to the men," Mr. Logan said.

"I would bring a group of students from the high school to teach English to the Chinese. We will use basic primers, the same books we use to teach reading in the elementary school. I'm certain that in a few months they will all be able to communicate."

"And start Bible lessons," Reverend Winslow added.

Papa said, "Gentlemen, I think your idea is excellent. Why don't we start this Sunday?"

The men rose and shook hands. Molly turned her attention to the magazine. She didn't want to appear to be eavesdropping. But her mind wasn't on the pictures. Charles would certainly be working with his father, and Betsey would want to teach in order to be close to him. Molly wanted to teach, too; she liked the idea of getting to know one of the Chinese men. Perhaps her student would tell her stories about China and she could write them in her diary.

The next day the children went to school. When they came home, there was milk and gingerbread on the kitchen table for them. Willie was breaking his cake square into tiny pieces as Betsey and Molly came into the room.

"How was school?" Molly asked Willie.

"I hate school."

"Why?"

"Nobody wanted to play with me," Willie said sadly.

"I know how you feel," Molly said.

"How was your day?" Mama asked them as she entered the kitchen.

Willie made a sour face. The girls didn't answer.

"Tomorrow will be better," Mama said sympathetically. "I'm sure it will."

"I think Papa's project is wonderful," Betsey began.

"What project, dear?"

"Teaching Sunday School to the Chinese men, of course. What a charitable thing to do...helping to convert them to Christianity."

"Your father isn't converting them. In fact, he is allowing them to construct a special room for their own religion on the grounds," Mama said.

"But Reverend Winslow is planning to teach them English and Bible stories. Isn't that God's work?"

"In a way," Mama said. "And you want to teach, am I right?"

Betsey nodded.

"Is Charles Winslow teaching?"

Betsey nodded again. This time she smiled and blushed.

"Betsey, I know you want to be with

Charles," Mama said.

Betsey lowered her eyes. Molly saw her sister turn pale and the smile fade.

"It's all right. I understand." She patted her daughter's hand. "You can teach on Sundays after church," Mama said.

"Oh, Mama, thank you." Betsey's smile returned.

"Your father and I had a long talk about the Chinese men, and I promised him that I'd try to be more understanding of their difficulties and..." she hesitated, "...differences."

"I'd like to teach, too," Molly added quickly. "May I, Mama?"

"Yes, dear," Mama said. "I don't see why not."

After church, there was a meeting in Papa's study with the Reverend and the volunteer teachers.

Reverend Winslow passed out primers. "I've discussed the best method for teaching English with Mr. Logan from the elementary school. You'll be using the First Primer and pictures from magazines. If you have any problems with a student, Mr. Logan will assist you. You'll each be assigned one man to work with for half an hour. Then small groups will be formed to start simple conversations."

Mr. Logan addressed the group and suggested that the teachers speak slowly and try to use simple words. He advised, "Use your hands to try to express ideas."

"Under no circumstances are you to touch the men," the Reverend instructed.

Johnny Sing gave a list of names to the Reverend. The Reverend then wrote the names on small white cards, one name to a card, and then distributed them, giving one card to each person in the room.

Reverend Winslow handed a card to Molly. On it was written "Chen Li."

Betsey and Molly walked with the volunteers to the factory.

It was a warm, sunny day with the only shade coming from the shadows of the wooden fence that enclosed the factory courtyard. Several rows of benches were set up in the center of the courtyard.

Molly waited nervously for the men to arrive. One by one they appeared, in clean cloth suits similar to the ones they were wearing when they got off the train. Mr. Sing announced their names. The volunteer teacher then raised his or her hand, and the student went up to the teacher.

"Chen Li," Mr. Sing called.

Molly raised her hand, and a young man walked toward her. Molly shaded her eyes in order to see him better, but it wasn't until he was in front of her that she realized he was the same young man whose eyes she had met at the train depot.

"My name is Chen Li," he said in English, and he bowed his head.

Molly didn't know whether to bow or not. She decided to do a quick curtsy. "My name is Molly Bartlett." Molly pointed to herself. "Miss Bartlett." She blushed. Then she gestured toward the benches, and Chen Li followed her to one of the empty ones. He pointed at the sun. "Hot!" Then he lifted the bench and carried it to a shady corner. He remained standing until Molly sat down.

Molly and Chen Li sat next to each other. Molly studied him as she handed him the primer. His face was round, with high cheekbones, his eyes were hazel (not dark brown as she had originally thought), and his hair was dark and straight, and it was pulled into a pigtail that reached to the middle of his back. He looked to be about Betsey's age, or maybe a little older.

"So you speak English?" she asked.

"Little, Miss Bartlett," he said.

"Good." Molly smiled. Chen Li looked away quickly.

He's shy, Molly thought. That's nice.

"Book. Primer." She pointed to the name on the cover. Then she opened the book.

Chen Li repeated, "Book." Then he reached

into his wide sleeve and pulled out a small, worn book of Bible stories.

"I have book." He gently stroked it and showed it to Molly.

"Where did you get it?" Molly asked.

"English lady in China. She teach English to boys going to America."

"That's wonderful," Molly said with excitement.

"Wonderful?"

"Wonderful means good...more than good. It's wonderful that you studied English."

"Wonderful I studied English. I want to read books." He tucked the book back into his sleeve.

Molly opened the first page of the primer. There was a big letter "A" and an apple. "This is an apple." Molly pointed.

Chen Li smiled and nodded his head. "Apple is in my book."

He opened to the first story about the Garden of Eden and pointed to the picture of Eve holding an apple in her hand.

"In the Bible it is not called 'apple.' It is called 'the forbidden fruit,'" Molly said. She turned the page of the primer. "..boat..cake.." Chen Li repeated the words on the page, and Molly put them into simple sentences. "The boat is big."

"I came to America in big boat," Chen Li

said.

"Very good," Molly said. "Is this book too easy?" She started to close the primer.

Chen Li frowned. "Please, I want to know more new words. Apple and boat I know. But no cake in Bible stories!"

Molly opened the book again and continued.

At exactly half past the hour, Reverend Winslow clapped his hands and announced, "The individual instruction period is over." Then he read aloud a passage from the Bible.

Mr. Logan organized small groups for conversation practice. Mr. Logan and Johnny Sing addressed the groups and explained the exercise in English and Chinese. Chen Li had no difficulty conversing in English.

"My name Chen Li," he said in response to the question. "I come from Kwontong, China. I went to San Francisco with my Uncle Wu."

CHAPTER THREE
"Why Did You Accept a Gift From a Stranger?"

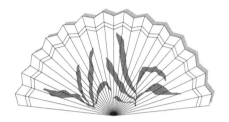

In the weeks that followed, Molly taught Chen Li every Sunday afternoon. Each night she wrote in her diary.

Kevin, our driver, drove over the bridge and past the factory on the way to school today. I saw Chen Li inside the courtyard. I waved to him, but he lowered his eyes. There were only a few strikers marching in front of the iron gates at Papa's factory.

The next week Molly noted:

Chen Li smiled at me today when I waved to him from the carriage. He was cleaning vegetables in the courtyard.

It was the first warm day of spring. The family had returned from church and had finished a cold lunch. Betsey had changed into her new summer frock, mail-ordered from Boston. "What do you think?" Betsey twirled to show off the full skirt. "Blue is Charles's favorite color." She was very happy these days. Charles had apologized profusely for not meeting her when he had promised, and he was as attentive as ever. He had explained that his teacher had kept him after school that day and he couldn't let her know because she had not been in school. His father had kept him busy with chores in the days following, but now he was free to be with her.

"You look beautiful," Molly said. She was still wearing her winter skirts and cotton shirtwaists.

"Mama said I can wear my hair up this summer," Betsey said proudly.

"Really? You're so lucky. I hate my curls." Molly twisted the one escaping from her headband.

"Maybe when you're in high school, Mama will let you wear yours up, too," Betsey reassured her.

"I hope so."

"Charles is going to ask permission to formally court me. Reverend Winslow does not agree with Papa about bringing Orientals into North Adams, but he does agree with the lessons on Sunday."

"Oh, Betsey, how exciting! Do you think Mama and Papa will allow Charles to court you?"

Betsey crossed her fingers. "I hope so."

The sisters walked hand in hand to the garden behind the kitchen.

Mama was picking tulips. Molly saw Charles waiting for Betsey at the bottom of the steep gravel path near the back of the gardener's cottage. When Betsey waved, he started up the hill toward the garden.

Charles, dressed in his Sunday suit, had come straight from church. He was tall and slender, with narrow shoulders and straight dark hair parted neatly in the center.

"Molly, tell Mr. Logan that we will be late," Betsey said. "We're going to talk to Mama now."

Molly walked down the path toward the road. "Good luck, Charles," she said with a smile as they passed. Charles, looking very serious, only nodded.

Molly wondered what her parents would say about Charles courting Betsey. Mama knew Betsey was in love, but Papa was too busy with the factory to notice how often she talked about Charles.

Molly started to think about Chen Li. What did he want to do when his contract was over? He had told Molly that he wanted to stay in America, but what could he do for a living? The Chinese were not allowed to become citizens. Until her father had brought the men to North Adams, Molly had never heard of a Chinese man who didn't work on the railroad or in the mines.

Chen Li was waiting for Molly at the entrance to the courtyard.

He bowed his head. "How is Miss Bartlett?"

"I am fine, Chen Li. How was your week?"

"It was very busy." They walked to a small bench in the shady corner of the courtyard. He bowed his head again and waited for Molly to sit first. Then he reached into his wide sleeve and pulled out a long, thin package wrapped in brown paper and tied with a string.

"Miss Bartlett, it is for you."

"For me?

"Yes. It will make you cool in the sun." Chen Li smiled as he handed her the gift.

Molly slowly opened the package. Inside was a fan. She carefully pulled apart the thin ivory supports and spread the paper folds. The fan was painted with pale, delicate flowers. "It's beautiful!" she exclaimed with pleasure.

"I give you the fan. I made it for you. Thank you for teaching me."

Molly started to fan herself. "Thank you." She blushed. Chen Li sat down next to her, and for a few seconds neither one spoke.

Molly fanned herself quickly. "We have to start now. Do you have the book?"

"Yes," Chen Li said. He pulled out the collection of short stories he was reading. "I have made a list of new words."

"Good," Molly said, as she continued to fan herself. The last word on Chen Li's list was "wedding." After explaining the meaning, Molly found herself telling Chen Li about Betsey's plans.

"Sixteen is old for a girl to marry in China," Chen Li said. "My sisters were...what is word?...promised, when they were very little. Family makes the arrangements. The girl goes to live in the house of her husband's family. Will your sister go to live in Reverend Winslow's house?"

"No. They will have their own house," Molly said.

"I will save my wages and when I marry, I will buy a house," Chen Li said proudly.

"In China?" Molly asked.

Chen Li hesitated. "There is no future in China for me."

"But don't all the Chinese men have to go back to China?"

"I will save my money."

Mr. Logan interrupted them and asked Chen Li to join the conversation group. He was in the most advanced one.

Later, when Molly arrived home, she showed her mother the fan.

"Why did you accept a gift from a stranger?"

her mother demanded.

"Chen Li isn't a stranger," Molly protested. "I thought it was very thoughtful of him." She fanned herself. "It really helps in the hot weather."

"You must give it back to him next Sunday," Mama said firmly.

"Why?" Molly was puzzled.

"Because a young lady does not accept gifts from a man, especially..." Mama stopped herself.

"Mama, he's just a student who wanted me to be comfortable. It's very hot in the courtyard."

"If it's so uncomfortable there, then don't go. You are a young woman of breeding. You do not accept gifts from anyone outside of the family. Do you understand?"

"Yes, Mama, but I still don't understand why it's so wrong."

"It is not proper. The fan is to be returned," Mama answered sternly.

Molly went to her room, threw herself on her bed, and looked at the fan. The flowers were hand-painted with watercolors. Each stroke was a delicate wisp. Molly didn't want to return it to Chen Li. She was certain he would be offended, and besides, she loved it.

Molly gently fanned herself and thought of Chen Li. He likes me, and this is his way of telling me he's my friend. Molly wrapped the fan in a lace handkerchief and hid it under her mattress.

Suddenly, Betsey burst into the room. Molly could tell from her sister's smile that everything had gone well.

"Mama said that Charles can come calling!" Betsey announced excitedly.

"And Papa?"

"Mama said she'd talk to him tonight, but I shouldn't worry." Betsey hugged her sister.

"That's great news, Betsey," Molly said. She wished she could share her secret with Betsey, but she was afraid her sister wouldn't understand her desire to keep the fan. You like a Chinese man? You must be crazy, Betsey would probably say.

"We'll get engaged next Christmas and married next June," Betsey continued. "Will you be my maid of honor?"

"Oh yes," Molly said excitedly. "I'd love to be your maid of honor."

"Wonderful!" Betsey danced around. "I want a white and yellow wedding with daisies and daffodils in my bouquet. And Molly, you'll wear flowers in your hair. You'll look beautiful."

Molly let her sister chatter on. Instead of listening, she thought about Chen Li and the fan.

CHAPTER FOUR
"It Is the Land of Gold Mountains"

Molly waited impatiently for Sunday. Late Friday morning, she went to Peterson's General Store with Betsey to help her choose fabric for her wedding trousseau. Of course, Mama would have the final word, but she was busy with household duties this morning.

Mr. Peterson cut off a square of ecru cloth. "This is a sample of fine silk so that you can decide what threads you will need and practice your stitching patterns," he said.

"Isn't this beautiful?" Betsey exclaimed, as she pulled another bolt from the shelves.

"Come on, Betsey," Molly said. "It's as hot in here as the kitchen on baking day. Let's come back later when it's cooled off."

"What you ladies need are fans," Mr.

Peterson said, as he reached under the counter and placed two lovely fans in front of them.

"Oh, these fans are very beautiful. Did they come from China?" Betsey asked. Two other customers turned to admire the fans.

"A young Chinese man brought them into the store to sell." Mr. Peterson spread one of the fans wide to show the hand-painted design.

"They're lovely," Molly breathed, a secret smile on her face. She wished she could tell Betsey about her gift.

"If only I had extra money, Mr. Peterson, I'd buy the fan," Betsey said.

"Perhaps next time," Mr. Peterson replied.

"I'm ready," Betsey said as she placed samples of cloth and thread in her wicker basket. Kevin was waiting in the carriage to drive them home. It was too hot to walk the half-mile up Chase Hill.

When they arrived home, Molly went directly into her room and took the fan from under her mattress. It was the same size as the others, but the design was different and even more beautiful. Her fan had many more flowers and a colorful butterfly on it. Perhaps Mama will let me keep it now that Chen Li is selling them at the general store, she thought.

After dinner, Molly told Mama about the fans she had seen at the general store.

"Chen Li painted them," Molly added proudly. "Since they're sold at the store, won't you let me keep mine?"

"A bought fan is one thing," Mama announced, "and a gift fan is quite another."

On Sunday Chen Li waited for Molly at the usual place—the entrance to the courtyard. He was holding the book of fairy tales she had lent him to read during the week.

"Hello, Chen Li," Molly called when she saw him. The hot June air and the dust from the yard made her lungs burn. She started to cough as they walked to their special bench in the shady corner of the yard.

"It is a good day to use a fan," Chen Li suggested without looking at Molly. She cleared her throat.

"Yes. I'm afraid I left the fan at home," she said softly. "I saw your fans at the general store. They were beautiful."

"Thank you, Miss Bartlett. I hope to earn money. Johnny Sing will take fans to other general stores to sell. Maybe he will take them to Springfield and Boston."

"That would be wonderful!"

"Wonderful. That is the first word you taught me."

"Yes." Molly remembered and blushed.

For a few moments they didn't speak. Then she took out her teaching materials.

"I've been reading Jane Austen," she told Chen Li. "She wrote *Pride and Prejudice.*"

"I did not know there were lady writers," Chen Li said.

"Oh, yes, there are," Molly answered. "And now you know a lady writer...me. I'm going to be a writer." Molly reached into a knit bag at her side and pulled out a notebook. "I wrote a story about you and your uncle. It's called 'The Trip to the Golden Mountains.'" Molly handed the notebook to Chen Li.

"I cannot read this," he said as he looked down at the writing.

"Why?"

"I do not know these letters," Chen Li admitted.

"I forgot. It's in script, and you have only been reading print. We'll read it together."

"It is something I must learn," he said.

"You'll learn script writing quickly. You're the best student at the factory," Molly said confidently.

"Because you are the best teacher," Chen Li answered instantly.

Molly blushed again and began to read her

story aloud.

"Inscribed on the gatepost of Chen Li's family house was the motto, 'May Five Blessings Come from Heaven.' The white plaster house with a roof of gray tile was blessed with many generations of Wu and Li families, but the spirit of prosperity had not smiled on them."

"Excuse me," Chen Li said as he put his finger on the word "Li." "My family name is Chen, my given name is Li."

"Wu and Chen families." Molly changed the name, and continued reading.

"No one from the street could see the family crowded into the center room, which served as the kitchen, dining room, and gathering place."

"How do you know all of this?" Chen Li interrupted.

"You told me. We talked about houses and how different my house is from your home in China."

Chen Li studied the writing as Molly read.

"'There is gold everywhere in California,' Uncle Wu bragged to the family. 'When Chen Li and I return to Kwontong, we'll have enough gold to make the family wealthy.'

"'Yes,' nodded Chen Li's revered grandfather. 'It is the land of Gold Mountains, Gum San.'

"Grandfather took a silk purse out of his

wide sleeve. The coins clanked as he released the drawstring around the pouch.

"'The family has saved fifty coins for your passage,' Grandfather said as he counted the money into the hand of his second son, Uncle Wu. 'This is for your voyage.' Then he counted out ten extra coins. 'Until the good spirits lead you to your fortune, you will have needs.'

"Grandfather gestured to Chen Li. 'Grandson! You will bring honor to our family and return to us with good fortune.' He counted fifty-five coins.

"Chen Li bowed his head.

"That night the women sewed the coins into the lining of the travelers' tunics.

"The next day Chen Li and his uncle left for Hong Kong, and by the next full moon they were passengers on a ship to America, the land of Golden Mountains."

Molly closed the notebook. "You must tell me more so that I can continue the story."

"I will try. The books I read about America did not tell the truth. I thought there would be many jobs, and houses for everyone," Chen Li said bitterly.

"What was it like when you arrived in San Francisco?"

Chen Li looked sad. "We lived in an old

boardinghouse with many men from our village. Every morning we went to an agent to try to get work. There were long lines and no work. Many days we had no money for food." The expression on Chen Li's face changed to determination. "I will make my fortune in America. In China you get job and house from your father. My father is a weaver of carpets. It is an honored craft, but there were too many sons and no future for fourth son. In America I can get job and house myself. I want to be a merchant. The future is in buying and selling. I will work hard," Chen Li explained. He took a deep breath after his long speech. "My fans are only the beginning."

"You will be a success," Molly said. "I feel it."

"And you will be a great writer like Jane Austen," Chen Li added happily.

Mr. Logan interrupted the lesson. "Molly, please tell Chen Li about July Fourth and the Revolution. Your father is going to allow the men to go to the celebration in town."

"I know about your July Fourth," Chen Li said proudly.

"You do?" Mr. Logan looked surprised.

"Johnny Sing told me the story of the Boston Tea Party and the Revolution. We do not like to pay tax on tea in China, either! Someday there will be a revolution there, too, but I will be in America."

Molly smiled, "Yes, and you will have good fortune."

Chen Li returned Molly's smile, only more broadly, and with his eyes beaming.

CHAPTER FIVE
"We Both Have Dreams"

Molly and Betsey spent the morning of July Fourth preparing their picnic lunch of cold chicken, biscuits, potato salad, and fruit.

"Are you going to give the fan back to that boy?" Betsey whispered as she packed the fruit into the wicker basket. The night before, Molly had told her sister all about the gift and Mama's reaction.

"He made it for me and I want to keep it," Molly answered defiantly.

"You're blushing!" Betsey laughed. "You like him." Betsey was surprised. "How could you! He's nothing but a dumb coolie."

"No! He's not dumb! He's very smart! I'd like to see you learn Chinese as quickly as he's learning English. And don't call him a 'coolie.' He has a name—Chen Li."

"Why do you like him so much?"

Molly hesitated. "He's...he's interesting. He's not like anyone around here."

"You're right about that. Why did he come here?"

"Chen Li came here with his uncle because they needed to work," Molly explained.

"He's lucky he didn't have to come alone," Betsey commented. "How did he get the contract to work at the factory?" she asked as she tasted the potato salad.

"Chen Li had a book of Bible stories in English in his sleeve and when Papa saw it, he spoke to him directly."

"Papa picked Chen Li himself?" Betsey seemed impressed.

"Yes, because he could speak some English."

"I thought the agent hired the men for Papa," Betsey said. "How old is he?"

"Sixteen," Molly answered. "He works as an assistant in the kitchen with Johnny Sing, and he's learning to use the sewing machine. He hopes that selling the fans will help him earn money for his future."

"Back in China," Betsey added.

"Chen Li wants to stay in America. He wants to be a merchant."

"A Chinese merchant! Nobody will buy from

him." Betsey laughed.

Molly felt her cheeks redden again. "Betsey, please don't say anything to Mama. If she knew I liked Chen Li, she wouldn't allow me to teach him on Sundays."

"I won't. After all, you didn't tell on me when I sneaked out to see Charles."

"Anyone home?" a male voice called from the back door.

"Charles, you're early," Betsey replied. She wiped her hands on her apron and pulled it off. "How do I look?" she whispered to her sister.

"Beautiful."

Betsey hugged her. "Someday you'll have a proper beau courting you."

Molly, Betsey, Willie and Charles walked down Chase Hill and across the Hoosac River bridge. When they got into town, they saw American flags hanging from buildings and stores, and even in front of private homes. Red, white, and blue streamers were tied around the lampposts, and flower-filled pots decorated windows and porches everywhere they looked.

The young people walked up the hill to Colegrove Park and found a spot to set out their blanket and wicker baskets. They were early for the celebration; only a few families were unpacking their lunches at the picnic tables near the children's playground. Betsey and Charles announced that they were going for a walk.

"Can I come?" Willie begged.

"No," Betsey said sweetly. "Charles and I want to be alone."

"We'll do something together," Molly suggested.

"I want to fly my kite over at the ridge," Willie said.

"All right," Molly agreed.

As they walked through the playground to the grassy ridge that sloped down toward East Main Street, Molly saw the back of a man dressed in a new cotton suit. He wore a pigtail that was held at the bottom by a red strip of fabric. Chen Li had once told her the pigtail was called a "queue." The young man was holding a kite string and jerking it back and forth over his head to take advantage of the air current. Molly knew instantly that it was Chen Li.

Willie ran ahead and stopped just to the right of Chen Li. Molly slowly followed her brother. She watched Chen Li as he concentrated on flying his kite. He was smiling as he manipulated the cord holding the large, green, dragon kite.

"Molly, will you help me with my kite?" Willie called.

"What?" Molly was preoccupied.

"Will you help me get my kite up?" he repeated.

"I'm really not very good at kite flying," she said finally. "Maybe Mr. Chen can help you."

Chen Li turned when he heard his name. He looked surprised. Molly smiled shyly.

"Chen Li, this is my brother, William Bartlett, but everyone calls him Willie. Willie, this is Mr. Chen Li."

Chen Li bowed his head.

"Your kite is beautiful, Chen Li." Willie pointed to the green dragon flying across the clear, blue North Adams sky.

"I made it," Chen Li said proudly.

"You sure got it to go up high!" Willie said with admiration.

Chen Li nodded. "I will help you."

He wrapped his cord around a tree branch and helped Willie unwind his lead cord. Molly watched as Willie chattered about kites, and Chen Li explained about air currents. Before long, Willie's kite was flying.

"Thank you for helping Willie," Molly said.

"You are welcome, Miss Bartlett."

"Please call me Molly."

Chen Li hesitated, smiled, and slowly bowed his head.

"I am honored...Molly."

"Did you fly kites in China?" Molly asked.

"Yes. There are many kites in China. Men and boys fly them. In America I see only boys fly them." He looked up at his kite and the serene expression returned to his face.

"Beautiful blue sky...and those..."

"Clouds," Molly added.

"Yes. The sky and clouds are the same in China. I miss China today. We have many celebrations. Your July Fourth reminds me of our New Year."

"When I visited my aunt in Boston, I was homesick, too," Molly said sympathetically.

"I am not sick," Chen Li replied quickly.

"Homesick doesn't mean sick sick. You are sad inside for China. You miss home. We call that homesick."

"Yes. I understand now. Please sit," he suggested. They sat next to each other and leaned their backs against an oak tree.

"I like North Adams, but I miss home," Chen Li said, breaking the silence.

"I understand."

"I do not like sleeping in the factory. In China, we have a house. My grandparents, parents, aunts, uncles, brothers, and unmarried sisters all live in a big house. I want to live in a house, too."

"And I want to have my own house, too,

someday. And I want to be a famous writer. We both have dreams."

"Dreams?"

"Yes. Plans. Hopes. I have dreams. I want to fly like a kite," Molly added, looking up at the sky.

"I understand," Chen Li said. "I want to fly like a kite, too."

Molly and Chen Li watched the two kites flying across the clear sky. Neither spoke. Then Chen Li said aloud, "I would like you to be my friend."

"You are my friend," Molly answered.

CHAPTER SIX
"Rumors Ruin a Young Lady's Reputation"

To Molly, Sunday had become the most important day of the week. She always carefully planned what she would wear and prepared the weekly lesson for Chen Li.

She was looking in the mirror and pulling back the outer corners of her eyes to see how she would look if she were Chinese when Willie pushed open the door.

"Chink! Chink!"

Molly quickly dropped her hands. "Don't say that. It's a nasty word to call someone. Where did you hear it?"

"The boys at school. They said the Chinks are strikebreakers," Willie explained.

"I guess they are breaking the strike, but calling them Chinks isn't nice."

"Sorry."

"Accepted. Now out of my room, Willie."

The relationship between the Chinese workers and the people of North Adam had mellowed slightly during the summer, and the furor died down. Reporters stopped trying to interview Molly's father. Ministers invited the Chinese to their Sunday services, and soon it wasn't unusual to see clusters of neatly dressed Chinese men sitting quietly in the last row of every church in town.

In August, Chen Li started writing notes to Molly. He told her not to open the letters until she was home.

Molly read the first one. He wrote how much their friendship meant to him.

The days are long until Sunday. I wait for my friend, and when I see her, I am happy.

In another letter, Chen Li told her that he was moving to a rooming house near the factory, and that his fans were selling at general stores in Williamstown, Cheshire, and Pittsfield.

Molly placed the letter with the fan under her mattress. There were now five letters there, all tied together with a pink satin ribbon.

She answered the letters by asking simple questions about China. She never wrote anything personal.

The first day of school was as hot as midsummer. Molly was in eighth grade, and she was relieved to find the girls more interested in her sister's engagement than the strike at the factory. She carefully avoided the subject when she ate lunch with her friends, Louise and Mary Jane. After school she walked home alone.

Molly was on her way upstairs when Mama appeared in the doorway to the music room.

"Molly, come in here, please. I want to speak to you."

Molly followed Mama into the music room and sat across from her.

"I am very disappointed in you," Mama said. She reached into her basket and pulled out the fan and the bundle of letters from Chen Li. "I was helping Beatrice turn your mattress, and I found these." She paused and stared at Molly. "What do you have to say for yourself, Molly?"

Molly couldn't breathe. Her clenched hands turned white. "The fan was a gift from Mr. Chen because I was helping him learn English," she stammered.

"We discussed the fan last June, and I told you to return it."

Molly nodded, miserable.

"You disobeyed me," Mama said sternly.

"I couldn't return the fan. It was a gift."

"Do not answer me back, young lady! Would you explain these letters from Mr. Chen?" Mama held the letters.

"He was practicing writing English. They are not personal letters," Molly tried to explain.

"They *are* personal letters, and he addressed you by your first name."

Molly's eyes started to well up with tears.

"What is going on between you and Mr. Chen?" her mother asked.

"Nothing, Mama. I teach him English on Sunday."

"You used to teach him English on Sunday. You are never to go near the Chinese men again — Mr. Chen or anyone else. Your relationship with Mr. Chen could start rumors. And rumors ruin a young lady's reputation. We do not want to have a scandal."

"But Mama, Mr. Chen and I are just friends."

"Friends. You don't make friends with Orientals. They are not our kind!" Mama almost shouted. Molly had never heard so much anger in her mother's voice before.

"Mama, please..."

"You are to come home directly from school and stay in your room until I am satisfied that you understand how I feel. And, as for Sunday, you will go to church with the family and come straight home afterwards. Do you understand?"

"Yes, Mama." Tears ran down Molly's face.

"Now go to your room, Molly!"

Molly ran upstairs to her room and threw herself on the bed, sobbing. The more she wept, the angrier she became. I can't just stop seeing Chen Li without telling him why, she thought. It would be a cruel thing to do. I have to see him one more time, even if I'm caught and locked up in my room for the rest of my life.

CHAPTER SEVEN
"Is That the Sunset?"

"I have to see Chen Li," Molly said with determination as she and Betsey walked to school. "I'm going to stop in at the factory on my way home."

"I think that's a bad idea," Betsey said. "Papa will see you and tell Mama, and you'll really get in trouble!"

"I suppose you're right," Molly agreed, reluctantly.

"When I'm out walking with Charles, I sometimes see Chen Li flying his kite in the park. Maybe you could meet him there, and no one would know."

Molly hugged her sister. "That's a wonderful idea! But how do I get out of the house?" Molly wondered aloud.

"You could say you have to do homework with a friend," Betsey suggested.

"Mama would just say that I'm too young to go out at night and I have to do it on the weekend. No, I have to think of something else."

The girls walked on in silence.

"If I could get Mama and Papa out of the house for the evening, then they wouldn't know that I was gone," Molly said.

"That's it," Betsey said. "If you can wait until Thursday, I heard there's going to be a meeting at the church to talk about housing the men outside of the factory. Reverend Winslow asked Mama and Papa to attend."

"Perfect. I just hope they'll go!"

"And Charles and I will walk to the park each evening until we see Chen Li. I'll tell him that you may be at the park on Thursday," Betsey added.

The days dragged on until Thursday. At dinner, nothing was said about the church meeting.

"Molly, stop playing with your food," Mama said.

Molly put down her fork and looked anxiously at her sister. Betsey picked up the cue immediately.

"How long do you think the meeting will be?" Betsey asked.

"Probably quite long," Papa said. "As you

know, your future father-in-law likes to talk."

"I'm afraid people will be angry about your plan to move the Chinese men into rooming houses in town," Mama said.

"I hope not. It's a good plan," Papa said. "It's time for them to live with other townspeople."

Molly waited until she heard the front door close. Then she grabbed her shawl and tiptoed down the back stairs so that Willie wouldn't hear her.

"Good luck," Betsey whispered from the crack in her bedroom door.

Daylight was fading. Molly ran down the path behind the garden. The hill was steep and, in her haste, she almost lost her footing before she reached the bottom of Chase Hill. She took a deep breath and smoothed out her clothing. She crossed the river, passed her father's factory, and walked quickly up Main Street to Cole Grove Park. Her heart was thumping. She pinched her cheeks to try to give them color, smoothed back her hair, and walked nervously into the park.

The playground was silent and the benches empty. As Molly walked further, she saw a figure in the distance. The figure turned. He was holding a kite, but he was not dressed in the familiar Chinese cotton suit. Instead, the man was wearing workman's trousers and a blue cotton shirt.

"Chen Li?" Molly called.

"Molly!" he said as he walked toward her.

"You look different," she said when they were standing together at the edge of the park overlooking the village.

"I traded kites for pants and shirt at Mr. Peterson's store." Chen Li turned around and Molly noticed that he had not cut off his long pigtail.

"I have moved with Uncle to the boarding house. We were the first to move because I can speak English. The other men have trouble."

"I know. My parents are at a meeting tonight to discuss housing outside the factory."

Molly looked away. Chen Li looked so happy, and now she was going to have to tell him why she had come to find him.

"I am glad to see you." Chen Li tied the kite string to a tree branch. "Let us walk." He looked at her. "Why are you sad?"

"My mother found your letters and the fan you gave me." Chen Li looked puzzled. Molly continued nervously. "She doesn't feel a lady should accept a gift from a man—a stranger. I didn't want to give you back the fan, so I hid it under my mattress."

"I am not a stranger." Chen Li was confused.

"I know we are friends, but my mother

doesn't. And the letters—she was very upset about the letters, too. She doesn't want me to be friends with a..."

"...a Chinese man," Chen Li finished.

Molly was afraid she was going to cry. "Mama doesn't want me to teach you on Sundays."

Chen Li's face grew stern. "Everyone in America came from another country, yes? In San Francisco, I meet men from Ireland, Italy, and Germany."

"Yes. In fact, the Bartlett family came from England," Molly answered. "I know it isn't fair. But coming from England is different than coming from China."

"Is it because we look different?" Chen Li asked.

Molly nodded. "I guess so. I feel awful about it." Molly turned away from Chen Li and looked down at the town of North Adams. The gas lights on the streets were lit. Then, almost as though a picture was coming into focus, a glow on the horizon caught Molly's attention.

"What's that?" Molly pointed in the direction of Marshall Street. There was a hazy orange ball. "Is that the sunset?" she asked.

"The sun sets in the west," Chen Li said. He pointed. "That is north."

Chen Li and Molly watched for a few seconds. Then they shouted together, "Fire!"

"The factory's on fire!" Molly turned and started running down the hill. "Fire! Fire!"

Chen Li followed. "I will get help," he shouted as he dashed past her.

"I'm coming, too," Molly said, and she ran after him.

CHAPTER EIGHT
"I Don't Know If We'll Have Enough Water!"

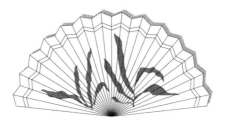

Molly and Chen Li ran down the hill from Cole Grove Park.

"I have to ring the fire gong," Molly said, as she continued running toward Main Street.

As Molly passed the general store, she saw Mr. Peterson rolling a barrel into his store.

"Fire!" Molly shouted as she ran by.

"What! Where?" he asked.

"My father's factory," she gasped.

"You're right. I see the smoke," he said, as he pulled off his white apron and jumped into his wagon. Two customers came out of the store and started running down the street.

"I'll ring the gong," Mr. Peterson called, as he lifted the reins. In seconds, he passed Molly.

Mr. Peterson was striking the big metal triangle when Molly arrived at the firehouse on Center Street. The clanging was as loud as the church bells. North Adams's volunteer firefighters started appearing on the streets.

"The fire's in the factory courtyard," Molly shouted. She doubled over and tried to catch her breath.

Fire Chief O'Mally and Mr. Peterson ran to the stable behind the firehouse and brought the horses out. As the other men arrived, they pulled out the pumper and hoses. Molly continued hitting the metal triangle.

"I'm not going to help save the factory of a man who hires strikebreakers," a man shouted.

"What if everyone refuses to fight the fire?" Molly asked Mr. Peterson, with tears in her eyes.

"If the Bartlett factory burns, then the fire could spread to the other buildings. You can't ignore a fire even if you don't like the policies of the owner of the property," Mr. Peterson said, loud enough for all the men to hear.

Molly hoped the others agreed with Mr. Peterson. Men were helping Fire Chief O'Mally hitch the team of two gray horses to the water pumper. Another wagon and more horses were readied to carry the equipment and volunteers.

"Fire's at the Bartlett Factory," Fire Chief O'Mally shouted above the sound of the gong.

A few men turned away from the wagon, saying, "Ain't gonna help that man!"

"Let his rotten factory burn!"

"Bartlett brought those heathens into this town to do our jobs," a burly man yelled.

Fire Chief O'Mally jumped into the driver's seat and took the reins.

"Please, may I ride with you?" Molly asked anxiously.

"It's against regulations," Fire Chief O'Mally said, "but climb up here!"

He pulled Molly up beside him. Molly looked back at the pumper and saw only a few men hanging onto the sides. The wagon holding the ladders, buckets, and hand equipment was following the pumper. It was only half filled with volunteers when it pulled away from the firehouse.

"Do you think there are enough men to fight the fire, Mr. O'Mally?" she asked anxiously.

"I don't know," he called, as he whipped the horses to full speed. Molly held onto the side of her seat. She could see smoke rising from the direction of Marshall Street. "I can't see the orange light I saw from the hillside!"

"The wall around the factory is blocking your view, but I smell the smoke," he said. He cracked the whip over the horses' heads.

"There's my father's carriage!" Molly pointed

to the open carriage being driven by Kevin. Her father and grandfather were sitting in the back. When the pumper passed the carriage, Molly saw the shocked expression on her father's face when he recognized her. He pointed at Molly and yelled something, but she couldn't understand him.

The pumper pulled up to the factory entrance. The gates were opened and Molly could see the reflection of the flames on the windows. Fire Chief O'Mally pulled the horses to a stop. Instantly the pumper was surrounded by men, dozens of eager, helpful men. Molly realized that they were all Chinese!

Chen Li and Johnny Sing were the leaders; Uncle Wu was just behind them. Johnny shouted orders in Chinese, and before the wagon arrived, they were unrolling the hoses from a round wheel and pulling them into the courtyard. Other men were preparing to pump and waited for their orders.

Chief O'Mally was the only man dressed in an official uniform including hat, coat, and boots. He cupped his hands, raised them to his mouth, and shouted to the men, "We have to put out the fire and water down the wooden houses next to the factory, too."

"Why?" Molly asked Chief O'Mally, when he sat down to catch his breath.

"To keep the fire from spreading. Most of the buildings in North Adams are wood. Wood burns!"

The air was filled with black smoke. There was a heavy odor of wood burning, and the sounds of falling branches and trees. Molly's eyes stung and she coughed as she watched.

Molly saw her father walking through the crowd. He had taken off his jacket, rolled up his sleeves, and was joining the firefighters near the front end of the hose.

"Go home!" he shouted to her. Molly pretended not to hear him over the noise. She saw Chen Li relieving one of the town volunteers on the end of the pumper, and Kevin was replacing the other. Together they pushed the wooden bar up and down in tandem. On the other side of the pumper, there were two more volunteers seesawing the bar.

"Look! Look!" Chen Li shouted.

Molly and Chief O'Mally turned toward the men. Chen Li was pumping the bar with one hand and pointing frantically with the other. Chief O'Mally jumped down from his seat and ran to the huge, round water tank. Chen Li was again working the bar with both hands. Molly could tell from his face that something was wrong with the water barrel of the pumper. Kevin was talking to him. Then he began shouting.

"Leak! Water leak!" Kevin said.

"Yes. Water is coming out of the side of the barrel," Chen Li shouted.

"What's wrong?" Papa shouted as he raced toward the pumper.

"There's a water leak, Mr. Bartlett," Chief O'Mally said. His voice was grave as he shook his head from side to side. "I don't know if we'll have enough pressure to pump the water."

Molly's father looked desperate. "We have to do something!" Papa shouted.

"I can fix the leak," Chen Li yelled over the noise and confusion. He shouted something in Chinese, and another young Chinese man took his place at the pumper bar.

"I have special thin wood from China. I use it to make kites. I can fix the leak."

"The pumper has to be fixed from inside. Can you fix it without emptying out the water?" Mr. O'Mally asked.

"Yes, I can," Chen Li said quickly.

"Let him try," Mr. Bartlett said.

"I will get my kite tools." Chen Li ran down the street toward his rooming house.

Papa's face was tight from worry and frustration. He kicked the wheel of the pumper.

"We'll have to organize a bucket brigade." Chief O'Mally shouted to the men between his cupped hands, "Men, start forming a line down to the river!"

Molly watched Johnny Sing walk over to her father and say something. Then her father told Chief O'Mally to tell his men to listen to Johnny Sing. Johnny climbed up on the pumper and started giving orders in Chinese.

Every one of the Chinese men became motionless as Johnny's voice cut through the turbulence. Then they sprang into action, rushing toward the wagon, and taking buckets from under it. They ran to their places in the newly formed line. Within minutes, a human chain reached from the factory across Marshall Street and down to the banks of the Hoosac River.

Men, women, and older children who were watching the fire from across the street filled in wherever they could find a space.

Papa was examining the leak when Chen Li returned, carrying a small painted box. Sweat ran down his face.

"I will fix the barrel," Chen Li said breathlessly.

"I don't see how," Chief O'Mally said, "but give it a try, boy."

"I'm going to lose everything," Papa said, staring at the dripping pumper.

Molly jumped down from the seat and

walked over to the pumper to get a better view.

Chen Li took out a thin piece of wood. "This is special wood I use for kite," Chen Li explained. He cut a strip and pushed it into the leaking seam. Then he used a wooden mallet to pound it into the space. "When wood gets wet, it gets bigger."

Chief O'Mally touched the repair. "It's still leaking."

Chen Li took a jar of glue and a small paint brush out of his box and dabbed the area where the leak was. "This will close the leak. See? No leak!"

The three men touched the area and cupped their hands to wait for water.

"It worked! Chen Li, it worked!" Molly shouted, and started to jump up and down.

"Come on, men, keep pumping. We should have enough water now for the factory and the houses," Chief O'Mally said.

The bucket brigade was working smoothly. Full buckets of water were passed forward from person to person, and empty buckets were passed back to the river. Johnny Sing started a second line of buckets to the house next to the factory. The men climbed to the roof and wet the house down. Another line of men filled the pumper so that there would be a steady flow directed toward the fire.

Chen Li went back to working the pumper. When the fire was contained and finally put out,

Molly saw her father and grandfather walk into the courtyard area to survey the damage. There was still smoke, but the worst was over.

"All clear! The fire is out!" Chief O'Mally shouted, and Johnny Sing repeated the words in Chinese.

A joyous cheer filled the night.

"Beer's on me," Mr. Smith, the owner of the Lion's Head Tavern, shouted to the workers. His barmaids rolled out a keg of beer into the middle of Marshall Street, and Chinese and American fire-fighters were offered a mug of the brew.

"Where is the young man who fixed the water pumper?" Papa shouted.

Chen Li stepped forward.

A smile spread across Papa's face. He held out his hand to Chen Li. "Thank you, young man. You may have saved my factory." They shook hands.

"And you probably saved a good portion of the houses on Marshall Street, too," Chief O'Mally added.

"Good work," Johnny Sing said in English.

Molly watched her father lift his mug high into the air. "I drink to you!" He drank from the mug. "I would like to reward you," Papa said. "What can I do for you, young man?"

Chen Li hesitated before he spoke. Then he

said quietly, "When I finish contract, I would like to stay in America."

"If you'd like to stay at the Bartlett Shoe Factory, there'll be a job for you."

"Thank you, sir, but..." Chen Li stammered. "I...I would like to work in a store. I would like to buy and sell."

"Hmmm..." Papa downed his beer, then said, "I will see if I can help you. I understand you have made beautiful fans and wish to sell them."

"Yes, Mr. Bartlett," Chen Li said.

Then Papa shook Chen Li's hand and surprised everyone by saying, "I'd like you to come to my house on Chase Hill for Sunday dinner."

Molly climbed into the carriage next to Kevin, their driver. Her father and grandfather sat in the back. "Kevin, thank you for your help with the fire," Papa said. Then he turned to Grandpa. "I'm going to need more men to help me get the factory back into shape. I'm impressed that the men in the union put aside their personal feelings and helped to save our factory. I'll see if they want to come back and work for me. I promise to make some changes—not all, mind you, but some. Perhaps we can work out our differences."

The carriage started to move. They passed Chen Li and Johnny Sing, and Molly and her father waved at them.

Soon the carriage turned into their driveway and Willie came running to meet them. "I could see the fire from my window," he shouted. "Tell me everything."

Mama was waiting anxiously on the front porch.

"Are you all right, Thomas?" she asked.

"Yes, dear."

"Molly? Papa?"

"We're fine, Catherine," Grandpa said as he climbed out of the carriage. "Stop fussing!"

"Was anyone hurt at the factory?" Mama asked.

"No, Catherine. This fire could have been a disaster, but Molly's Chinese friend helped save the day."

"You have a lot of explaining to do, young lady," Mama said to her.

Papa put his arm around Mama's shoulders. "I don't want you to be hard on Molly. Chen Li is a fine young man, and we shouldn't keep her from being his friend."

Molly explained, "I only wanted to see Chen Li tonight to say goodbye. I had to tell him why I couldn't see him on Sunday."

"I've invited Chen Li and Johnny Sing to Sunday dinner," Papa said.

Mama looked stunned. "Thomas, you've

invited two Chinese men to dinner?"

"Yes, Catherine, two fine men are coming to Sunday dinner," Papa repeated. He turned to Molly. "Molly, you can continue to teach Chen Li English. He is a bright lad."

Molly went up to her room and looked out the window. She could see lights around the factory, but no fire. Then she took out her diary and wrote until the reflection from the moon told her it was very late.

The next day when she awoke, Molly found the letters and fan from Chen Li on her night table. "Thank you, Mama," Molly whispered.

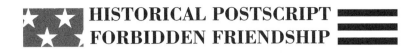

HISTORICAL POSTSCRIPT
FORBIDDEN FRIENDSHIP

Although the story of Molly Bartlett and Chen Li is fictional, it is based on actual historical events. North Adams *was* a small industrial town in the heart of the Berkshire Mountains. And there *was* a shoe factory there in 1870. The workers did strike, and Calvin Sampson, the owner of the factory, brought in Chinese workers from California to replace them. The rest, however, is a

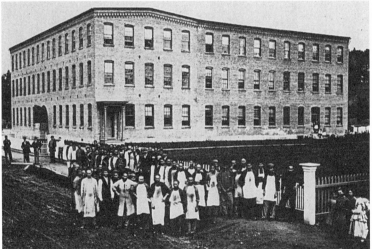

Courtesy of the Society for the Preservation of New England Antiquities.

Workers—many of them Chinese—gather outside Calvin Sampson's shoe factory in North Adams, Massachusetts.

different story — different from *Forbidden Friendship.*

Sampson's Shoe Factory

Calvin Sampson built his shoe factory in North Adams in 1863. By 1870, his three-story factory on Marshall Street had 200 workers and was producing 7,000 pairs of shoes a week. Sampson was a popular man in North Adams, which was then home to 12,000 people. He and his wife lived in The Wilson House, an exclusive boarding establishment. They had no children.

At the same time that Sampson was building up his factory, a strong shoemakers' union called the Secret Order of the Knights of St. Crispin was also growing. It had been formed to protect the rights of factory workers and to obtain fair wages. In 1870, the "Crispins" organized a strike among Sampson's shoemakers.

The Crispins demanded an eight-hour day. This was the first time in America a union was attempting to shorten the standard ten-hour day. The union also wanted an increase in salary from $1.70 a day to $2.00 a day, as well as the right to inspect the owner's accounts for profit.

Sampson was outraged by these demands. He would not give in. He remembered reading that a Chinese labor force had been brought in to break a strike in California, so he decided to bring Chinese workers to North Adams.

Chinese Workers

Since 1860, Chinese men in great numbers had been leaving their country to work overseas. Life in China had become unbearable. After paying taxes and rent for their farms, the people had no money left for food. They came to America to find work to support their families. China did not permit its people to settle in foreign countries, but it did allow them to work there on a temporary basis.

One of the Chinese workers at Sampson's shoe factory poses for a portrait in his traditional clothing.

At this time, the Chinese made up more than three-fourths of the workforce in some California factories. It was not an easy life for them. People were angry because they felt jobs were being taken away from Americans. Laws were passed to try to force the Chinese to leave the United States.

Other laws tried to limit the number of Chinese coming into the country. The government in California even declared a legal holiday for anti-Chinese demonstrations.

Breaking the Strike

Seventy-five of the men from China agreed to go to work for the Sampson shoe factory in Massachusetts. They would work for $23.00 a month. The Crispins had been paid $46.00.

Sampson had anticipated trouble from the

Another shoe factory worker, dressed in "American" clothing, sits for a photo.

townspeople, and it came! An angry mob waited on the train platform in North Adams. Police tried desperately to control the hostile crowd. Some men in the mob carried weapons.

As the train stopped, Sampson (armed with six pistols under his coat) jumped onto the plat-

Courtesy of the Society for the Preservation of New England Antiquities.

North Adams, Massachusetts was a busy New England town when this photo was taken at the end of the nineteenth century. The photo is taken from Witt's Ledge.

form and confronted the crowd. But no one moved when he ordered the crowd to "make way." Once Sampson repeated himself, however, the crowd grew silent and moved aside to let Sampson and the Chinese men pass. The factory owner and seventy-five Chinese men walked from the train station toward Marshall Street and the factory.

The factory grounds had been remodeled to accommodate the new workers. A high wooden fence had been built around the entire structure.

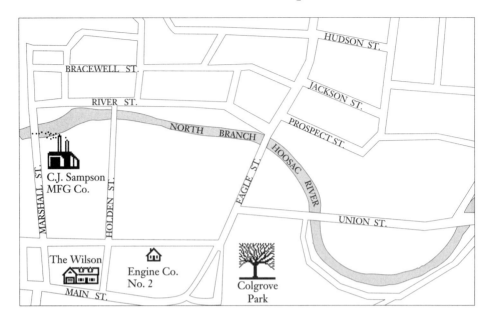

This map of North Adams shows the location of Sampson's Shoe Factory, his boarding house, the firehouse, and Colgrove Park in the 1870s.

A dormitory had been constructed, complete with dining room and kitchen. A fifty-foot plot, inside the fence, had been set aside so that the Chinese men could exercise outdoors.

The Chinese men proved to be excellent workers, but they had a hard time with the townspeople. Because of local hostility, the Chinese were not able to leave the factory compound for almost six months. Attempts were made to burn them out, they were unsuccessful. Although Sampson received several death threats, he was never harmed. Eventually, the Chinese completely replaced the strikers.

Staying in North Adams

Time passed. For ten years the Sampson factory was staffed by Chinese workers. Each group returned to China after three years, and another group took its place. As each man went home, he brought with him an average of $2,000 for his labors. This was a small fortune in China.

After ten years, a new generation of North Adams workers began to replace the Chinese, and the events that had begun on June 13, 1870, began to fade into history.

Other Books in the Stories of the States

Fire in the Valley
Voyage of the Half Moon
by Tracey West

Golden Quest
East Side Story
by Bonnie Bader

Drums at Saratoga by Lisa Banim

This manuscript was funded in part by a grant from the Massachusetts Arts Lottery as administered by the Northern Berkshire Council of the Arts, December 1989.

Special thanks to the North Adams Historical Society, the North Adams Public Library, the Williamstown Public Library, the Adams Free Library, Lillian Glickman, Roberta Immerman, Linda Neville, and Eugene Michalenko.

Forbidden Friendship is dedicated to Roberta Immerman, a good friend and a gifted teacher, and the children of the Plunkett School in Adams, Massachusetts.

J   98001545
Weber, Judith Eichler
Forbidden friendship

OLD CHARLES TOWN LIBRARY

CHARLES TOWN, WV 25414

DEMCO